Crispin
and the
3 Little Piglets

HELLO! MY NAME IS

Cheezy Mouse™

I WANT TO BE YOUR FRIEND
PLEASE LUV ME

WARNING: The name CHEEZY MOUSE™ and the heart-shaped ID badge
are protected by the trademark and copyright act of 1988.
Removal of this ID badge and renaming this toy
will destroy its market value
and render it
WORTHLESS

CRISPIN AND THE 3 LITTLE PIGLETS
A DOUBLEDAY BOOK 0385 603290

Published in Great Britain by Doubleday,
an imprint of Random House Children's Books

This edition published 2002

1 3 5 7 9 10 8 6 4 2

Copyright © Ted Dewan 2002

Designed by Ian Butterworth

The right of Ted Dewan to be identified as the author and illustrator of this work has
been asserted in accordance with the Copyright, Designs and Patents Act 1988

Papers used by Random House Children's Books are natural, recyclable products made
from wood grown in sustainable forests. The manufacturing processes conform to the
environmental regulations of the country of origin.

RANDOM HOUSE CHILDREN'S BOOKS
61-63 Uxbridge Rd, London W5 5SA
A division of The Random House Group Ltd.

RANDOM HOUSE AUSTRALIA (PTY) LTD
20 Alfred Street, Milsons Point, Sydney,
New South Wales 2061, Australia

RANDOM HOUSE NEW ZEALAND LTD
18 Poland Road, Glenfield, Auckland 10, New Zealand

RANDOM HOUSE (PTY) LTD
Endulini, 5A Jubilee Road, Parktown 2193, South Africa

THE RANDOM HOUSE GROUP Limited Reg. No. 954009
www.kidsatrandomhouse.co.uk

A CIP catalogue record for this book is available from the British Library.

Printed and bound in Singapore

Crispin
and the
3 Little Piglets

cyber psnail

KARAOKE KID
Sing-a-long Sound System

Good Vibrations

Oscillating
Slumber Sling

ASSEMBLED IN AFGHANISTAN
UNDER STRICT UN SUPERVISION

Swan
Lake
Scented
Nappy
Disposal
System

Lil·Bo·Peep
CCTV
Monitor

homeopathic
ultrasound
suspension
babybather

sterila

3

Ted
Dewan

DOUBLEDAY

To the triplets,
Patrick, Kyle, and Matthew

This little paper house
is for you guys

Crispin Tamworth was a pig who had it all
to himself.

He had loads
of stuff to
play with,

and two
best friends,
Penny and Nick.

One day, Mrs Tamworth said to Crispin, "How would you like a little brother or sister?"

"Why would I want one of those?" asked Crispin.

"Oh, you'll like it when the time comes," grunted Mr Tamworth.

But Crispin
wasn't sure
he wanted
a new piglet.

His friend,
Penny, had
little brothers
and sisters.
So Crispin went
over to Penny's
house to see what
it might
be like when
the time came.

There were an awful lot of them,
but it looked like fun.

After he left
Penny's house,
Crispin thought
it might be nice
to have a
little brother
or sister
to play with.

After all, there
would only be
one of them.

Finally the time came. Mrs Peck, the housekeeper, took Crispin to the hospital where Mr and Mrs Tamworth were staying.

"Look, Crispin," said Mrs Tamworth. "Aren't they sweet?"

Three little piglets were wriggling in their blankets.

The first piglet
made a mess
all over
Crispin's shirt.

The second
piglet just
screamed and
screamed.

But the third
piglet was quiet
and cuddly.
"I'll take this one,"
said Crispin.

But Crispin was
very surprised
when all three
little piglets
came back to
his house.

Next day, Aunt and Uncle Potbelly came over with a great big CHEEZY MOUSE™ for Crispin.

Then they hurried away to play with the piglets.

Paula from next door came over with a great big CHEEZY MOUSE™ for Crispin.

But then she nipped away to play with the piglets.

Finally, Nick's dad came over with a great big CHEEZY MOUSE™ for Crispin.

But even *Nick's dad* slipped away to play with the piglets.

It just wasn't fair.

When the
3 Little Piglets
made a great big mess,
everybody said,
"Aren't they cute?"

Little Pigs! Little Pigs! Let me come in! Not by the hair on my chinny-chin-chin!

So Crispin made
a great big mess
and said,
"Look!
I'm a little
piglet, too!"

He was sent outside.

It just wasn't *fair.*

When the 3 Little Piglets
screamed and cried,
everybody said,
"Ooo, the poor dears,"
and played their favourite song.

Then I'll huff and I'll puff and I'll blow your house down

But when Crispin
screamed and cried,
saying, "Help me! I'm a
little piglet, too, and I
want a different song,"

he was sent outside.

One day, when the piglets were listening
to their Big Bad Wolf song for
the hundredth time, Mrs Tamworth said,

"Oh, Crispin,
I'm so busy and tired ...
won't you *please* keep
the 3 Little Piglets
quiet for a while?"

So Crispin tried
to keep the
3 Little Piglets
quiet for
a while.

But soon
there was
trouble,

and
crying,

and he was sent outside.

The next day, Nick came over.

"I hate the 3 Little Piglets," grumbled Crispin. "I hate their stupid Big Bad Wolf song."

"Crispin's afraid of the Big Bad Wolf ... tra la la!" sang Nick.

"No, I'm not!" shouted Crispin. "*I'm* the BIG BAD WOLF! And I'll huff ... and I'll puff ...

and I'll *BLOW* your house down!"

BIG BAD WOLF
became Crispin's
favourite game.

Crispin, Nick and Penny were busy playing BIG BAD WOLF one day when Mrs Peck said, "These piglets keep getting under my feet. Won't you kids let them play with you?"

"Aw, they're too little to play BIG BAD WOLF," Crispin whined. "They'll just cry."

But Penny knew a few good games they could all play...
like **RACING FAST CARS.**

And EMERGENCY HOSPITAL.

And the 3 Little Piglets
didn't cry all afternoon.

But then Nick and Penny went home,
and Crispin didn't know
what to do.

He rubbed the hair
on his chinny-chin-chin.

Then he said,
"You want to hear your stupid
Big Bad Wolf song?"

Yes

Yes

Yes

So they all climbed up on the sofa.

And they huffed,
and they puffed ...

Things got a little
out of control.

Big Bad Wolf
and the 3
Little Piglets
were sent to
their rooms.

LITTLE
PIGS
KEEP
OUT

But Big Bad Wolf crept out
and knocked on the door of
the 3 Little Piglets whispering,

"LITTLE PIGS! LITTLE PIGS! LET ME COME IN ..."

and he read them
their favourite
story.